THE GIRL WITH A BRAVE HEART

A Tale from Tehran

To my children, Meshi and Noam — R. J.
To Alma, Ruth and Ada — V. M.

Barefoot Books
2067 Massachusetts Ave
Cambridge, MA 02140

Barefoot Books
29/30 Fitzroy Square
London, W1T 6LQ

Text copyright © 2010 by Rita Jahanforuz
Illustrations copyright © 2010 by Vali Mintzi
The moral rights of Rita Jahanforuz and Vali Mintzi have been asserted

First published in the United States of America by Barefoot Books, Inc
and in Great Britain by Barefoot Books, Ltd in 2013
This paperback edition first published in 2018

Graphic design by Louise Millar, London
Reproduction by B & P International, Hong Kong
Printed in China on 100% acid-free paper
This book was typeset in Centaur, Rowan Oak and Azola
The illustrations were prepared in gouache using transparent and opaque layers,
and were inspired by the vibrant hues of Middle Eastern markets

Paperback ISBN 978-1-84686-931-0

Library of Congress Cataloging-in-Publication Data
is available under LCCN 2012035835

British Cataloguing-in-Publication Data: a catalogue record for
this book is available from the British Library

Originally published in Hebrew by Kinneret Zmora-Bitan Publishing

5 7 9 8 6

THE GIRL WITH A BRAVE HEART

A Tale from Tehran

Written by Rita Jahanforuz

Illustrated by Vali Mintzi

Barefoot Books
step inside a story

ON a quiet street in the city of Tehran lived a little girl called Shiraz. Shiraz's mother had died when Shiraz was born, and soon afterwards, her father married again. His new wife had a daughter of her own, the same age as Shiraz. Her name was Monir, and the two girls grew up like sisters.

At first, all went well. The family lived happily together and Shiraz's stepmother treated her kindly. Then Shiraz's father died. Everything changed overnight. "Without your father

bringing home money every week, we cannot afford a maid," said the stepmother. "We need to save money. Shiraz, from now on, I'd like you to do the housework."

Shiraz no longer had time to see her friends or play outside. Instead, she spent her days cooking and cleaning, washing and ironing. She missed her father terribly, but she knew she could not bring him back.

This story starts one autumn day when Shiraz had finished all her chores: she had cleaned the house and washed and ironed the clothes. Whenever she had a little time to herself, Shiraz liked to go and sit on the balcony at the top of the house. On her knees lay a ball of wool she had found among the few things that her mother had left her.

She settled down to knit herself a winter sweater when, all of a sudden, a gust of wind blew the ball of wool off her lap and tossed it far beyond the balcony.

Shiraz leapt up and clung to the railing. She looked all around her, straining to see where the wind had thrown her ball of wool. And at last, she saw it, caught in the branches of a rosebush in one of the courtyards nearby.

"That's my mother's wool," Shiraz said to herself. "I must go and get it."

Shiraz shivered — and not just because she was cold. She studied the path from her home to the strange garden and set off to ask for her ball of wool back.

She knocked loudly on the front door. She waited, but there was no answer. She knocked again. After a long time, a small window in the top of the door opened just a slit and a pair of eyes stared down at her.

"What do you want?" asked an old lady's voice.

"Hello, my name is Shiraz. Please excuse me," Shiraz said nervously. "My ball of wool has fallen from our balcony into your garden. Please, could I have it back?"

The eyes looked Shiraz up and down suspiciously. "I will give you your wool, but on one condition," the old lady said. "You must do a few chores for me, jobs I cannot manage on my own. Then you will get your ball of wool back."

"That would be a pleasure!" Shiraz replied. She was used to hard work and all she wanted was to have her mother's wool.

The door creaked open, and an old lady with wild and dirty long hair appeared. She hadn't washed her face, her dress was filthy, and her nails were long and curved. Shiraz's heart beat fast. She wanted to run away. But she stayed where she was. "This old lady has kind eyes," Shiraz said to herself. "She looks scary, but I expect she has just forgotten how to look after herself properly."

"Are you coming in or not?" asked the old lady impatiently. Shiraz stepped slowly inside.

She could not believe how dirty and smelly the house was. The old lady showed her the way to the kitchen. Plates, cups, pots and pans, all crusty with rotten leftovers, were piled high in the sink. The old lady gave Shiraz a heavy hammer.

"I want you to smash all the dishes, and the draining board and the sink. Smash everything," she said. Then she left.

Shiraz took a look around and put the hammer down on a stool in the corner.

Then she set to work. She washed all the dishes, she scrubbed the sink, and she mopped the floor. Then she filled a pot of water, lit the fire and prepared soup with some vegetables that she had found in a basket in a cupboard.

When the kitchen was clean and tidy and everything in its right place, she went to look for the old lady. "I have finished," she said. The old lady looked around the kitchen without a word.

Then the old lady led Shiraz out into the garden.
Everything was neglected. The grass was long, and weeds and
brambles had sprung up among the shrubs and the flowers.
The soil was cracked and dry. The old lady gave Shiraz a
pair of heavy shears. "I want you to cut down all the flowers
and pull out their roots. Cut down the bushes too. Destroy
everything. I don't want anything left," she said as she turned
around and trudged back into the house.

Shiraz looked at the sad garden. Then she set to work. She pruned and trimmed the plants, pulled out the weeds and cut back the brambles. As she was working, she heard the faint sound of water trickling. She looked, and there between the bushes she found a rock that was damp with fresh water. "There must be a hidden spring under this rock," she thought. "If I can unblock the spring it will water the garden." The rock was heavy, but Shiraz managed to roll it back. The water found its way to the bushes, the flowers and the grass, and the thirsty plants began to look green and fresh again.

Shiraz called the old lady. "I've tidied the garden," she told her. The old lady looked at all the work Shiraz had done but she did not say a word.

Next, the old lady took Shiraz to her bedroom. "I have one more thing to ask before I give you back your ball of wool. Take these scissors and cut my hair. I don't need this long hair anymore."

Shiraz looked at the old lady's wild hair. First, she washed it. Now the old lady's hair hung gleaming and silver down her thin back. Then Shiraz found a brush. She braided the old lady's hair and pinned it up in a neat bun.

Now the house was calm and clean, and the old lady looked much happier. "Here is your wool," she told Shiraz. "Thank you for all you have done. On your way home, go through the back gate. You will find two pools — one has clear water, the other dark. Go into the clear pool first. Dive underwater three times. Then bathe in the dark pool. Dive three times and no more. Then you can go back home."

Shiraz thanked the old lady, took the ball of wool from her and went out through the back gate. Just as the old lady had said, she found two round pools. Shiraz plunged three times into the first pool and three times into the second pool. Then she went home.

As she knocked on her own front door, Shiraz remembered that she had gone out without telling anyone and that she had not made the dinner yet. "Oh no," she thought, "I'll be in such trouble." She started to tremble as she stood waiting for her stepmother to open the door. She knew she would be severely punished.

But it was Shiraz's stepsister, Monir, who came to the door. She smiled and asked Shiraz very politely, "How can I help you?"

"I'm sorry I'm so late…" Shiraz began.

"I beg your pardon, who are you?" asked Monir.

Shiraz was puzzled. "It's me, Shiraz. I'm so sorry I've been gone so long," she said.

Monir laughed. "How can you be Shiraz?" she said. "You don't look at all like her — you're far too beautiful!"

"Please," begged Shiraz. "Don't make fun of me. Just let me in. Your mother will be angry."

Monir turned and shouted for her mother.

Shiraz's stepmother came to the door. "What can I do for you?" she asked politely.

"Please don't tease me anymore," Shiraz pleaded. "I'll explain everything … please, let me in."

At last, Monir and her mother realized that the beautiful young woman really was Shiraz. They were full of questions. "Where have you been? How have you turned into such a beauty?" Shiraz told them everything.

The next day, Shiraz's stepmother went to the market and
came back with two bags full of wool. Shiraz showed her the
old lady's garden. Her stepmother began to throw the balls of
wool wildly in all directions. One ball flew through an open
window and into a bowl of porridge, another fell into a ball
game and was kicked high into a tree. Another knocked a
passerby on the head.

At last, one ball rolled into the old lady's garden. "There it
is!" she said excitedly to Monir.

"Off you go!" Shiraz's stepmother hissed at her daughter. "Do exactly what you're told. And don't be lazy or rude. Remember to dive into the pools on your way home. I have a feeling that's where the magic is." She hid behind a tree while Monir knocked at the door.

"Come on! Open the door, you old bag!" muttered Monir. She knocked again.

After a long time, a small window opened, and a pair of eyes stared out at her.

"What do you want?" asked an old lady's voice.

"My ball of wool has fallen into your garden, and I want it back," said Monir.

"First, you must do a few things for me. Then I will give it to you," said the voice.

"Fine, fine," agreed Monir impatiently.

The door opened and once more an old lady with wild and dirty long hair appeared. Monir pushed past her. "What do you want me to do?" she demanded. The old lady showed her into the dirty kitchen and gave her a heavy hammer.

"I want you to break all the dishes and the draining board and the sink. Break everything," the old lady said.

Monir didn't waste a second. She grabbed the hammer and smashed all the plates and cups and all the pots and pans. When she had finished she went to find the old lady. "I've done that job," she said.

The old lady looked at the kitchen without saying a word.

The old lady led Monir out into the garden. The bushes had grown wild again, the flowers had wilted, and the shrubs were full of brambles. "I want you to cut down all the flowers and pull them out," the old lady said and gave Monir a pair of heavy shears. "I don't want anything left to bloom," she added as she walked away.

Monir cut down everything. She hacked the flowers, the shrubs and the two trees. Not a single plant was left standing. When the garden was completely destroyed, she went to find the old lady. "There, that's done too," Monir said. The old lady looked at the garden but didn't say a word.

The old lady took Monir to her bedroom. "There is one more thing I need to ask you before I give you back your ball of wool. Take these scissors and cut my hair."

Monir cut the old lady's hair quickly and carelessly. When she had finished, she asked impatiently, "Now, what about the pools?" The lady looked at her reflection in the mirror and saw how short her hair was, and how badly cut.

"Yes, indeed, now you should go and find the pools. Go through the back gate. You will find two round pools. One has clear water and one has dark. Swim in the dark pool first and dive under its waters three times. Then swim in the clear pool and do the same. Three times, no more," the old lady reminded Monir, "Then you can go back home."

Monir ran to the back gate. She forgot all about the ball of
wool that the old lady had given back to her. She found the
two round pools and jumped into the dark pool three times.
Then she jumped into the pool with the clear water.
She dived under the water not three, but ten times.
"I'll stay in the water longer than Shiraz,"
she muttered. "That will make me
much more beautiful than her!"

The sun was starting to set and
Monir was still in the water. Her
skin was all wrinkled and she
began to shiver from the
cold. At last, she pulled
herself out and ran
home.

Monir knocked at her door. She thought about how beautiful she must look. How pleased her mother would be!

But when her mother came to the door, she snarled, "We don't answer the door for beggars," and she slammed the door in Monir's face.

Monir tried again.

"Stop bothering me, you disgusting creature!" her mother shouted this time.

"Mother, it's me," sobbed Monir.

At last, Monir's mother realized that this really was Monir standing at the door, even though she looked hideous. Her hair hung limply around her ears, her eyes were mean and small, and her skin was grey and rough. "Tell me, you ungrateful wretch!" she screamed at Shiraz. "You came back from the old lady's house looking more beautiful than before — how is it that Monir looks so different and so hideous?"

"I … I don't know …" Shiraz was staring at her sister, shocked by what she saw.

"Is there something you didn't tell us about your visit to the old lady?" shouted the mother.

"I told you everything," Shiraz answered.

"And you Monir, did you do exactly as you were told?"

"Yes, mother, I did exactly what she asked. She told me to destroy the kitchen, and I destroyed it. She told me to destroy the garden, and I destroyed it. She asked me to cut her hair, and I cut it."

The house fell silent.

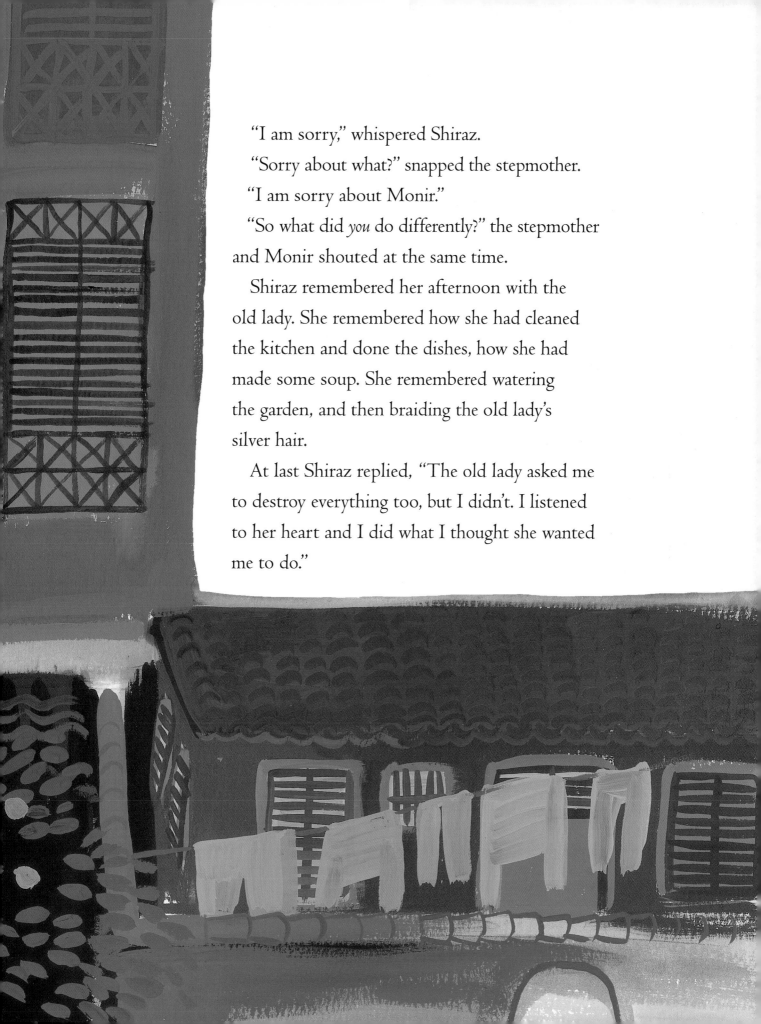

"I am sorry," whispered Shiraz.

"Sorry about what?" snapped the stepmother.

"I am sorry about Monir."

"So what did *you* do differently?" the stepmother and Monir shouted at the same time.

Shiraz remembered her afternoon with the old lady. She remembered how she had cleaned the kitchen and done the dishes, how she had made some soup. She remembered watering the garden, and then braiding the old lady's silver hair.

At last Shiraz replied, "The old lady asked me to destroy everything too, but I didn't. I listened to her heart and I did what I thought she wanted me to do."

Many years passed. Shiraz and Monir grew up. People found the hidden garden with its tangled bushes and overgrown trees. They found the two pools and tried swimming in them. And it was then that they discovered the old lady's secret magic.

Both the dark pool and the clear pool have the same water. They don't change the people who dip into them. They just make them look the way they feel on the inside.

And everyone remembered Shiraz, too — the girl with a brave heart, who had listened and had understood that when people are sad, they do not always know how to ask for what they need.